A.M. Walker

A Lecture on the Private and Literary Life of Burns

SALZWASSER VERLAG

A.M. Walker

A Lecture on the Private and Literary Life of Burns

Reprint of the original, first published in 1859.

1st Edition 2022 | ISBN: 978-3-37513-146-3

Verlag (Publisher): Salzwasser Verlag GmbH, Zeilweg 44, 60439 Frankfurt, Deutschland
Vertretungsberechtigt (Authorized to represent): E. Roepke, Zeilweg 44, 60439 Frankfurt, Deutschland
Druck (Print): Books on Demand GmbH, In de Tarpen 42, 22848 Norderstedt, Deutschland

A LECTURE

ON THE

PRIVATE AND LITERARY

LIFE OF BURNS;

PUBLISHED FOR THE BENEFIT OF THE

USEFUL KNOWLEDGE INSTITUTION.

BY

A. M. WALKER, M.A., M.D.

———

Tunbridge Wells:

PRINTED BY JOHN COLBRAN, HIGH STREET;
AND SOLD ALSO BY THE BOOKSELLERS.

—

MDCCCLVIII.

PREFACE.

As HONORARY SECRETARY to the Useful Knowledge Institution, I am naturally interested in its welfare and prosperity, and finding that no new Books have been added to the Library during the last five years, I publish this little work, in the hope that it may be instrumental in raising funds for the purchase of some of the best standard authors, — in which the Library is very deficient.

I, therefore, trust that the members,—the Gentry and Tradesmen of the Town, who are interested in the success of the Institution, will unite with me in promoting the sale of iv.

the edition ;—especially as its proceeds are to be handed over to the Treasurer, for the purpose I have mentioned.

This Lecture was delivered, by request, some years ago, before some of the Metropolitan Literary and Scientific Institutions.

Sussex House, Parade, Tunbridge Wells.

ROBERT BURNS is now, with most of us, a household word,—a word which we can never utter without recalling the best affections. It is sounded around hearths innumerable, and with immortal song it is consecrated in all that is most genial, most loving, and most loveable in our intercourse; in the freshness and fun of our laughing nature, and the sadness and sorrows of more thoughtful hours. It is unnecessary to dwell long on a life so well known, but the order of my subject requires that I should not entirely pass it over. If it be not new, it has at least an interest in the memories which can bear repetition.

He was, as most of you know, the son of a Scottish peasant, and born in 1759, in a cottage on the banks of the Doon. His father was no common man, and, if a peasant, he was of that order of peasant which makes his country's pride. According to his son, and all his son's biographers, he was a man of original and

B

vigorous mind, of extensive and useful information, of moveless integrity, of earnest and deep piety, and of solemn, even, austere manners. His mother is described as having all the softness and purity of her sex, mild, affectionate, and benignant. She loved her son, her home, her family, and her country; and she sung by her fire-side the olden ballads of her poetic and native soil, as well as became a matron of the land of "the Wallace and the Bruce." Robert seems a noble compound of both his parents,—the fine and manly clay of his father, attempered with the dewy tenderness of his mother,—the whole fraught with that Promethean fire, throbbing in his powerful and passionate soul, which *Coila*, the muse of his country, breathed into him when she kissed him in his infant cradle, and anointed him the immortal bard of her own loved Scotland.

Considering his circumstances, his education was, on the whole, a good one, and in reference to his poetic destiny, it may be well doubted whether it could be better. No college, it is true, could claim him as her son, but he was not on that account without an education. He knew not, to read a Latin oration, nor to scan a Greek verse; but he knew what was more to his purpose—to read the heart of man, and the works of God. We are not, however, of those, nor was he, who consider all things within the power of wild and untutored genius. Genius itself must be trained and elaborated into adequate expression, yet in a way suitable to its peculiar tendencies. Burns knew this with the strong wisdom which belongs to great minds, and he acted on this knowledge. He cultivated his intellect to the full extent of his opportunities; he neglected no means of instruction, and he despised no useful acquirement. He had none of that indolent vanity which delays preparation to the last, and then trusts all to sudden excitement and undigested emotions. He looked to the ideal, as every man of genius does, and he was aware that this was not to be discovered in a passing glance, or to be reached in a single bound: he knew that in the effort to unfold it, no execution could be too careful, and no labor too great; and he felt, that justice to himself, and respect to his art, demanded an honest and earnest devotion of his powers.

The most conspicuous characteristics of true genius, is the constancy and even the fastidiousness with which it struggles to perfect every faculty, and to unite industry with inspiration. The man of genius appreciates the sacredness of the work whereunto he is called, and he dares not rush to it with a spirit unprepared. It is not the consciousness of power, but the conceit of vanity, which trusts entirely to momentary impulses, and which mistakes the contortions of a delirious imbecility for the movements of a potent inspiration. There is no error more fatal, no delusion more ruinous, than the idea that native endowment has little need of preparatory study. Without profound and patient thought no great work has ever been produced; and the creator of immortality has never been an ignorant man.

Even in the works of God we observe preparation and progression: the earth on which we stand, so fair to look upon, so robed in beauty, and so radiant with life and light, has sprung from a chaos through innumerable formations; and even the thunder

which seems so sudden in its burst, and the
lightning that appears so rapid in its flash,
are but the rush of materials of comparatively
long and slow accumulation.

Any view of genius which dispenses with
the necessity of labor, I regard as of most
pernicious influence. For genius, as it appears
to me, has two essential properties, corres-
pondent and needful to each other. The
first is, an innate capacity of emotion and
conception; the second is, the capacity of
transferring them to others. Allow me to
illustrate this position a little more in detail.
Take, as examples, some of the most prominent
developments of what we term " genius."
Genius in the poet implies a deep knowledge
of the inward life of man, with its varied
feelings and aspirings, united to a fine sensibility for all that is grand or beautiful
in the outward creation; in the orator, an
acquaintance with human passions, and the
means of moving them to a purpose; in the
actor, a subtle discrimination of character and
the mode of realizing it; in the painter, a
perception of truth, grandeur, or beauty, as

manifested in color, form, and position; in the sculptor, an apprehension of grace or majesty, independently of color, and exhibited merely in shape and attitude. So far we have stated but one essential, and our view is yet vague and imperfect: one form of genius is not thus absolutely distinguished from another, and in some of the points noticed they are all identical. It is the mode of expression, that in each completes the idea, and defines its boundary. As to the inward power, all species of genius has much in common; it is in their developments we have their peculiar distinctions. The genius of the poet expresses itself in measured language; of the orator, in language unmeasured; of the actor, in voice, look, and gesture; of the painter, in the living canvass; and of the sculptor, in the breathing statue. Here, then, we have the invisible inspiration and the outward sign; the invisble inspiration which gives the objects of it existence only to the soul of the inspired; the outward sign, which gives them existence also in the minds of others.

We may then term these two elements of genius the ideal and the artistical; the ideal in relation to the conception; the artistical in relation to the execution. Both of these can be only made excellent by labor; and the history of all great productions shows that they cost their authors exceeding toil. This is the general fact, and the exceptions are inconsiderable. How many a cast does the sculptor mould before his vision is fixed in the shape of beauty, and his eye gazes on that over which he long had dreamed?—how many a rough sketch is thrown from the painter's hand, before the canvass dawns into that living eloquence which reveals the ethereal creatures of his imagination?—how deeply, how thoroughly, and how anxiously does the orator collect and arrange his materials, before they are hurled forth in that electric torrent which shall set a multitude of minds on fire? How zealous therefore must he be whose art, above all these, is the most glorious and the most enduring! The man of genius is at once the most fervent enthusiast and the most subtle analyser; and every noble production is but an embodiment of the highest logic. To gain lasting effect on mankind there must be truth and power of combination; truth and power of combination demand knowledge; and knowledge requires study and reflection. Genius is not intoxication, and it is even more than enthusiasm. It is the capacity to invent or to create; and invention implies the clearest discrimination, and creation the highest art. The flash of noble thought may come suddenly on the brain; the torrent of mighty passion may burst upon the heart; but the spirit of order must move ere it is shaped into that beauty which the world does not willingly let die. The importance of the principle I have endeavoured to expound, and the admirable illustration it has received in our poet, are the apology I plead for the introduction of these remarks.

Burns relatively to his destiny, as I have already said, was in the highest sense educated;—educated by his mother's voice and by his father's care;—educated in home, where at night the daily toil was forgotten around the " clean hearth-stane," and where the generous but " wee bit ingle " revealed nothing but happy and confiding faces : and there was that mother with her song and tale of other days ; and there were those children that looked with wondering eyes, and heard with devouring ears ; and there was the father, who entered into all their griefs and gladness, but allowed no tear or laugh to ruffle his solemn and weather-beaten face ;—their friend, their guardian, and their priest,—who worked for them and prayed for them,—read from the " big-ha " Bible, and offered up their morning and evening sacrifice to heaven. And Burns was also educated in one of those parochial schools which have made Scotland what she is—" the land that has risen in her eagle flight in the blaze of every science, with an eye that never winks, and a wing that never tires." Whatever many may think of the austere John Knox, it is immortal honor to his memory and wisdom that he placed such schools on every mountain and in every valley of his country,—schools which, from his time to ours, have been the nurseries of genius and of glory. Best of all, Burns was educated in his own spirit, that spirit which had early learned to pierce the surface of its emotions; to feel all joyous and all sorrowful affections; to feel " the passions' maddening play," and too often to be whirled in their wild convulsions : he was educated in the historic and poetic love of his country; from the hour his memory dawned, the music of sweet sounds was upon his ear, and the images of glorious deeds were in his fancy; the thoughts of " olden greatness arose on his meditations," and the shades of departed heroes thronged his solitude. He was educated in social intercourse and living sympathies; he loved his fellows, and he loved to be among them; his was no monkish genius, which moved ever amidst unpeopled streams and woods, and had no pleasure in the haunts of men; his was a large heart of powerful pulse, which sought for others to return its throb and to share its fulness; he looked at human life, at once with the eye of sympathy and discrimination, with the warmth of a poet and the sagacity of a philosopher : he was often amidst the throng of men, and much concerned in whatever brought them together, whether in melancholy or in merriment. And, lastly, he was educated in the glorious works of God; and though mere description has but a small share in his poetry, —that the grand and beautiful appearances of creation were congenial to his taste, and fed his imagination, we may know from his own words: "There is," he says, "scarcely any earthly object gives me more—I do not know that I should call it pleasure—but something which exalts me, which enraptures me, than to walk in the sheltered side of a wood or high plantation in a cloudy winter's day, and hear the stormy wind howling among the trees, and roving over the plain. It is my best season for devotion—my mind is rapt up in a kind of enthusiasm to him, who, in the ponderous language of the Hebrew Bard, 'walks on the wings of the wind.'"

I have spoken of our poet's love of knowledge. Like all noble minds, he had also a desire to extend it. Accordingly, we find him, while working on a cold and unprofitable farm, harassed with cares and struggling with difficulties, establishing a Book-club, forming its rules, and presiding over its arrangements. Dr. Currie, one of the most elegant, and even eloquent, of his biographers, makes some slight hints on the inexpediency of such refined studies to the working classes, to which Allan Cunningham offers a needless opposition. The day of controversy is now over, and, at present, to attack the opponents of popular enlightenment, is thrice to slay the slain. The people will have knowledge for themselves; and let other folks, if it please them, make argument against it.

The principle was never more forcibly stated than by Dr. Johnson, in one of his immortal conversations : " Sir," said the great moralist, " while knowledge is a distinction, those who are possessed of it will naturally rise above those who are not. Merely to read and write was a distinction at first,—when reading and writing have become general, the common people keep their places ; and so, were the higher attainments to become general, the effect would be the same." While I am on this topic, allow me to make allusion to a common maxim, as false as it is flippant. It is this: "A little knowledge is a dangerous thing!" A small measure of knowledge may truly be dangerous, when it puffs up the mind with silly and pedantic conceit; yet the danger is not great, for there is always a number of keen observers, sufficiently sharp to detect the pretender, and sufficiently severe to punish the presumption. It is dangerous to make a small share of knowledge do the work of a larger, as it is to make five pounds do the business of ten; but this does not alter the value of the five as far as they go;—and so every quantity of knowledge has a real worth proportioned to its extent. A little knowledge is often turned to good account. One instance occurs to me. When Mr. Crabbe in starvation and despair called on Mr. Burke, the orator knew of no means by which he could permanently serve him, except getting him into the Church. Poor Crabbe had but a mere smattering of Latin; yet Burke told him it was well he had that little; and so it was: it enabled him to receive ordination; ordination gave him literary leisure and permanent support; and these procured for the world his immortal tales.　　　　　　　　　　c

I am no advocate for superficial acquirement; yet such is the injustice of the world, that the lighter arts are commonly rewarded profusely, while profound science often fails to secure its possessor a subsistence. Mrs. Inchbald represents this with much point in the opening of her beautiful story, " Nature and Art." William the scholar of ponderous learning, unable to procure bread to stay his hunger,—Henry, the other brother, suddenly acquires patronage and wealth; and what could Henry do? He could play upon the fiddle !

After all, the knowledge which we can use in the ordinary course of life must of necessity be limited; and the most learned philosopher can no more bear all his science in his brain, than a wealthy merchant could carry his whole capital in his pocket. For common use both must have a supply of small change ; and there is no more danger to the commonwealth of literature by the diffusion of popular science, than to the commonwealth of society by the coinage of ten and five-penny pieces. Let there be rich men, and let them rejoice in their riches; let there be great men, and let them be proud in their greatness; let there be men of strong intellect, but let them in their strength be merciful: yet I have my doubts whether it is ever the great, the noble, or the strong, that are of destructive natures,—and this, more especially, is my impression, when I remember—it was the lean kine of Egypt that devoured all the fat ones. Analogously is it in literature; it is the poor, lean, hungry animals of the *critic species*, that are the most unsparing and the most ferocious. It is well for society that there should always be men of massive and mighty acquirements; but it is well also that the results of such acquirements should be extensively distributed. If it be good to have deep and full fountains, it is because they throw out their fulness and clearness into the sunshine; it is because they not only swell into the broad and gorgeous river, but also steal into the quiet streamlet, and give beauty to the secluded nook.

Let us now return for a brief space to the history of our poet. It can serve no useful or generous purpose to enlarge upon his youthful follies : they were mortal, and mouldered with his ashes in an early grave; but his genius, which was deathless, is with us, an everlasting energy. That his muse went hand in hand with his passions must indeed be confessed ; nor can it be denied that the inspiration of the one was often* reckless amidst the maddening play of the other. With characteristic ardour and with more zeal than wisdom he embroiled himself in the theological squabbles of the times; and by the destructive boldness of satire, and the shafted power of his ridicule, created against himself an enmity that followed him to the grave. In the thoughtless prodigality of wit and wildness, poor Burns called up a tempest which he had no magic to allay; he sowed the storm and he reaped the whirlwind; and justice compels us to admit, that the humor of the Bard was frequently unsparing against sentiments which, whether true or false, were sacred to many a heart. The world is witness, that of all enmities, those which religious irritation creates are the deepest, the most unsparing, and the least relenting. Earthly infirmity can pardon earthly infirmity ; but in the conflict of sectarian rancour there is no heart for pity and no room for tears. The poet's true mission is to humanity ; for the sake therefore of his own peace, for the sake of his glorious vocation, he should keep himself aloof from the clangor and the clashings of infuriated sectarianism.

That in such a man as Burns there should be a world of passion, and that in such a story as his it should have left some of the saddest and sublimest records, is no matter of wonder. And so it was. We see him at school in his far-off mountains, and by the solitary ocean, nominally learning mensuration, but in reality quaffing strong drink with smugglers, and talking love with a Highland lassie ; we see him, even before his boyhood passed away, toiling beyond his might; up early, and late at rest, helping his aged and struggling father ; in his short hours' repose his aching head upon his burning hand, and his over-worked heart palpitating to fainting or suffocation. We see him occupying a room in the little town of Irvine, paying a shilling a week rent, living upon oat-meal, working as a flax-dresser, and with that mixture of merriment and melancholy which followed him through life; giving a welcome carousal to the new year; having his shop burned to ashes, and being left—as he himself expresses it, like a true poet—not worth a single sixpence:—we see him, while death saved his father from the horrors of a jail, toiling with his orphaned brothers and sisters and widowed mother, on a barren profitless farm; and so, if we observe in the youth of Burns the germs of many misfortunes, which darkened his maturity and planted poisoned arrows on the pillow of his early death, we find also in his youth the most affecting evidences of his manly and noble nature. He was not a man that either sinned callously or suffered meanly; and if any one could plead circumstances in excuse for error, he was privileged to plead them. "The great misfortune of my life," he says, "was to want an aim. The only two openings by which I could

enter the temple of fortune, was by the gate
of niggardly economy, or the path of little
chicanering bargain-making. The first is so
contracted an aperture I never could squeeze
myself into; the last I always hated,—there
was contamination in the very embrace. Thus
abandoned of aim or view in life, with a
strong appetite for sociability, as well from
native hilarity as from pride of observation
and remark, a constitutional melancholy or
hypochondriacism that made me fly solitude;
add to these incentives my reputation for
bookish knowledge, a certain wild, logical
talent, and a strength of thought, something
like the rudiment of good sense, and it will
not seem surprising that I was generally a
welcome guest where I visited,—or any great
wonder that where two or three were met
together, there was I in the midst of them."

These remarks explain much of his subse-
quent life better than a thousand commentaries.
The same singular vicissitude of light and
shade, of glory and grief, is discernible in his
attachments. Burns had deep reverence for
woman, and he revered her as a poet. He

saw her in the light and joy of his own inspired heart. He threw around her the magic of inborn fancy, and saw in her the impersonation of all that he dreamed of the ideal, the fair, and the beautiful: he sought from her a sympathy for that full-fraught tide of life and passion that was too big for his own heart, and which should receive expression, or shatter the breast that held it. And Burns, in all untouched and natural simplicity, needed not high-born dames with the frontlet of gems on the robe of gold: enough for him was the brow which heaven itself had baptised with beauty: enough for him was the heart in which a generous nature beat with artless throbbings: the muse of his country had met him at the plough, and there was enough for him in the pleasant and handsome country girl to awaken the enthusiastic spirit of his song. Highland Mary, a rustic maid, was one with which his earliest romance commenced, and from whose memory the sun of that beautiful romance never departed. It was with her he departed, never to meet again, with cere-

monies congenial to his young and poetic
nature. In their last interview, he tells us,
they stood on either side of a stream, and
pledged their confidence with solemnities
which after circumstances have made more
interesting—they separated; a separation which
the early death of Mary made eternal. It is
the great power of genius—and most enviable
power it is—to make not only its passions
and caprice ours, but also its affections and
friends. Thus *we* feel—thus millions and
millions will feel towards Burns's Mary,
albeit she was only a fresh, handsome mountain girl, who, while living, trod unfearing
on her Highland heather,—and who, while
loving, lay without a dream of immortality
on the breast of her country's poet,—*now*,
while her grave remains almost unmarked,
obscure in a corner of Greenock churchyard,
her name breathes the whole passion of a
poet's heart, and lives with undying beauty
in the song of Burns. What memento could
her sainted spirit more desire than that
which he has wedded to immortal verse! I
refer especially to his poem—

"TO MARY IN HEAVEN.

"Thou ling'ring star, with less'ning ray,
Thou lov'st to greet the early morn,
Again thou usher'st in the day
My Mary from my soul was torn.
Oh Mary! dear departed shade!
Where is thy place of blissful rest?
See'st thou thy lover lowly laid?
Hear'st thou the groans that rend his breast?"

And so the poet continues through the whole of his heart-breathing composition, with a depth of pathos and a glow of inspiration, which sorrow, in its sweetest songs, has never yet surpassed—

"Still o'er these scenes my mem'ry wakes,
And fondly broods with miser care!
Time but th' impression stronger makes,
As streams their channels deeper wear.
My Mary, dear departed shade!
Where is thy blissful place of rest?
See'st thou thy lover lowly laid?
Hear'st thou the sigh that rends his breast?"

The scenery in which this was written was worthy of the thoughts with which it is inspired. It was composed under the blue and star-lit sky of a summer's night; under the arch of the broad calm heavens the poet lay, oppressed with a thousand passionate memories

—the realities gone for ever, but their shades
coming quick and fast over his excited imagination; it was in this way that Burns reclined in
his simple corn-field, and called up the dead
years and the buried joys, and gave them a
voice and music that shall ever be repeated
while language exists upon earth, and while
life and passion are in the heart of man.

This was the enthusiasm of a lover, but it was
also the enthusiasm of a poet; for it is he that
can realize and give fresh and speaking life to
those images that start up in his musings and
his day-dreams, and to those tones which sweep
over that vacancy of the soul, once a seeming
Paradise, which time and sorrow have trampled
to a wilderness. And, pardon me, if I pause
here to makè a brief but not inappropriate
reflection. It is remarkable that poetry, even
highest poetry—whose expression is so magical,
that from the earliest times it was considered a
gift from the skies—deals commonly with the
most simple emotions, and thus, while the bard
gives *these* true expressions, he utters the voice
of humanity, not merely of a thousand years,
but of its entire existence. Next to religion,

the poets are those whom Providence gives us to express the strongest wants of our nature. Religion affords a language to our aspirations for a hereafter; and poetry is the highest language of our experience here. Poor humanity, that would otherwise be like the dumb-child, agonized with wants without words, finds in the poet a friend, and an interpreter. Thus it is that prince and peasant, cottage maiden and courtly lady, all sing after their own fashion. In joy and sorrow, love and jealousy, in the bright and black passions of the world; in the comic and the tragic vicissitudes of life, from the dimlit-hut to the illuminated hall,—poetry is the revelation of musings which in the common life had no language, and of thoughts which lay too deep for tears. I have stated a principle, and a principle, I think, of very extensive range. For its illustration, I refer simply to Burns. How many a plain kirtled coarse-hooded country girl has the secret longings and sentiments of her worldless love impersonated in the Highland Mary! how many a sturdy and honest peasant has like feelings with him who immortalised his Nanny O!

whom neither moors nor mosses could deter
from seeing,—true to his trust, and troth as
noblest Knight that ever sought the balcony
of his lady-fair! How many a breast with
the same kind of anxiety as that of his "Poor,
but honest Soldier!" how many a ploughman
with a hand more coarse than Burns, and as
kind a heart, but without his heaven-touched
lips, might silently have moralised over "The
Mountain Daisy," or over "The wreck of
the Mouse's Nest!" And if they have never
so moralised before, his verses have taught
them that which was in them, but which
they knew not. Taking even the highest
order of poetry, how often have we all felt
it in our experience, but had no words to
furnish expression? The eloquence is in the
heart, but the tongue is chained. Who has
not felt it both in the joy and sadness of
life? How much of the comic and tragic of
emotion, of the romantic, the heroic, and the
ideal are buried in the depths of lowly and
unnoticed existence? Were it not so, the
poet's numbers would be an unknown tongue,
and when the trumpet gave forth an uncertain

D

sound, who should prepare himself to the battle? I have appealed to our experience for a proof of this unrevealed poetry that we all feel, and in confirmation, I may turn each in upon his own breast. How often we escape from real life, and how often we wish to escape from it, there is none of us who cannot testify. We seek infinite modes to accomplish it, and almost any mode is acceptable. Our youth, which was so bright a prophecy of hope, and which flings so luminous a shower of sunbeams over the spot on which even a negro sports,—*fades away :* that which is to all of us our romance, our poetry, departs, and instead there comes

> "Unwelcome visions of our former years—
> Till the eye, cheated, opens thick with tears."

Early as our poet went to the grave, there may be found in his writings sentiments answering to all these epochs in the human heart.

I turn now to a period of our author's personal and poetical history, which is at once painful and instructive. Jean is a name enshrined for ever in Scottish song. I shall not dwell upon the sad errors, or the blighting disappointments which clouded this portion of Burns's life. To have tarnished youth and innocence was, to a high and honorable mind, a terrible conviction; but to be hindered by the perverse austerity of a parent from making the only reparation in, his power, must have given the last sting to the bitterness of despair. But so it was. Armour, the father of Jean, would not permit his daughter to be the poet's wife; and in consequence, Burns was to become a deserted and a broken-hearted exile. Truly, the miseries of men of genius make a sad history! The first thought of publication was suggested to Burns to procure means for his expatriation. The first and little edition of his works in Kilmarnock slightly furnished his purse, but was highly creditable to himself and to his purchasers: to himself, that he put forth the noblest breathings of poetry,—to his purchasers, that though of the humblest classes, they proved their sympathy with that poetry by exhausting the edition. He realised, upon the whole, the pittance of twenty pounds; and whilst this was his all on earth, the roar of ocean that sounded of exile and foreign toil was already dreary and desolate on his ear. Mr. Cunningham, speaking of this part of his history, says :— "At that period ruin had him so effectually in the wind, that even food became scanty: a piece of oat-bread, and a bottle or two of penny ale, made his customary dinner when he was correcting the first edition of his immortal works,— and of this he was not always certain." But now approaches the crisis, both of his glory and his grief. An accidental call prevents his embarkation for America, a new suggestion leads him to Edinburgh, and rapid and brilliant as the lightning's flash he is born into fame. Fame, however, came before money. " When he dined out and supped," says Mr. Cunningham, " with the magnates of the land, he never wanted a monitor to warn him of the humility of his condition. When the company arose in the gilded or illuminated rooms, some of the fair guests, perhaps—

' Her Grace,
Whose flambeaux flash against the morning skies,
And gild our chamber ceilings as they pass.'

took the hesitating arm of the bard, went
smiling to her coach, waved a graceful good
night with her jewelled hand, and, departing
to her mansion, left him in the middle of the
street to grope his way through the dingy
alleys of the ' gude town ' to obscure lodgings,
with his share of a deal table, a sanded floor,
and a chaff-bed, at eighteen-pence a week."

These remarks evince the sensibility of the
biographer, but we have some doubt of their
justice. The lady may have been as free
from blame as the bard was from degradation.
The polished, and perhaps good-natured
Duchess, who was fascinated for an evening
with the witchery of Burns's eloquence, and
reflected on him in parting the glow which
his own enthusiasm had awakened, was, it
may be, ignorant of his distress—or, if not,
was too well-bred to notice it. But if Burns
was admonished of his humility of condition,
he never forgot the dignity of his manhood.
In the throng of Highland Chieftains and

Border Barons, in the full blaze of pride and beauty, he felt there was that within him superior to them all: in the inspiring grandeur of his poetry there was a power beyond the voice of heraldry: the muse of his country had crowned him with an unfading wreath: the patent of nobility was written in fire within his heart; and the great ones of earth became poor before the aristocracy of heaven!

No man paid more respect to rank and station, where respect was due, than Burns; but no man despised them more than when combined with ignorance, cowardice, or folly. The dignity of man in every station he ever upheld, and agreed with Pope, in believing *"an honest man's the noblest work of God,"* as he teaches us, for instance, in that truthful and vigorous song—

"FOR A' THAT, AND A' THAT.

"Is there, for honest poverty,
　　That hangs his head, and a' that?
The coward slave we pass him by,
　　We dare be poor for a' that!
For a' that, and a' that,
　　Our toil's obscure, and a' that,
The rank is but the guinea's stamp,
　　The man's the goud for a' that.

"What tho' on hamely fare we dine,
  Wear hoddin grey, and a' that;
Gie fools their silks, and knaves their wine,
  A man's a man for a' that;
For a' that, and a' that,
  Their tinsel show, and a' that;
The honest man, though e'er sae poor,
  Is king o' men for a' that.

"Ye see yon birkie, ca'd a lord,
  Wha struts and stares, and a' that;
Tho' hundreds worship at his word,
  He's but a coof for a' that:
For a' that, and a' that,
  His riband, star, and a' that,
The man of independent mind,
  He looks and laughs at a' that.

"A prince can mak a belted knight,
  A marquis, duke, and a' that:
But an honest man's aboon his might,
  Guid faith he maunna fa' that.
For a' that, and a' that,
  Their dignities, and a' that,
The pith o' sense, and pride o' worth,
  Are higher ranks than a' that.

"Then let us pray that come it may,
  As come it will for a' that,
That sense and worth, o'er a' the earth,
  May bear the gree, and a' that.
For a' that, and a' that,
  It's coming yet, for a' that,
That man to man, the warld o'er
  Shall brothers be for a' that!"

Little good and much evil did many of
these great folk do to poor Burns. The most

he ever brought away from them were intemperate habits, empty praise, vague expectations, and wounded feelings. When, after a little, he came a second time in contact with his aristocratic patrons, he found what stuff they were made of; and in their haughty formality and cold looks, he soon perceived what he had to expect at their hands. When the gloss of his novelty wore off, when he ceased to be a lion, and the fashion,—there was no charm in his wood-notes wild, and no magic in his native melody for the rank-loving coteries of the Modern Athens. He pierced the hollowness of elegant mediocrity, and he saw nothing to admire in a title, when it was but the nickname of a spendthrift, or in a star, when it only glittered on the breast of a tyrant, or a *roué*.

Burns went full of fame to see the highland glories of his native country. But now there were things more grateful to him than fame. He placed, at his own expense, a tomb over the neglected remains of his brother poet, Ferguson. He gave two hundred pounds from his small gainings to his brother Gilbert.

He met his affectionate mother with tears of
proud and honest joy in her widowed eyes.
He married his *Jean,* and granted peace to a
sorrowed and injured heart. " I have married
my Jean," he writes, " I had a long and
much - loved fellow - creature's happiness, or
misery, in my deposit, and I could not trifle
with such a trust!"

Misfortune, however, attends him. His toils
avail not. His farm is profitless; and his
money gone. In the mean-time, this noble
poet was made a guager; and finding guaging
and farming incompatible, he settled down to
his lot; he quits the plough for ever, to
measure casks during the remainder of his
short life. And amidst this measuring of
casks, and hunting of smugglers; amidst all
the crosses and cares of poverty; amidst all
the ills that suffering genius is heir to,—he
composes those songs, so eloquent in poetry
and passion, touching every chord—whether
in the boisterous laughter of joy, or in the
soft sad music of humanity.

Lonely, unfortunate, deserted, Burns every
day becomes worse. Every day brings its

weight of dead and dull calamity, bruising upon his heart, like the hag in the night-mare. He has sorrows that might bear down the most sensitive; and still worse, he has the peculiar sorrows of genius, with which few of the mass can feel. He incurs also the anger of his Government, and seeing promotion closed for ever, the prospect before him is but low drudgery for life. The lovers of despotism were offended at some breathings, scarcely audible, that escaped him in sympathy with the friends of liberty. The cry of France, in the mighty throes of her first revolution, reached his ear and aroused his heart, as it did all the souls of freemen; but the poor victim, with a wife and little ones that waited on his hand for bread, stifled the exultation in his throat. He saw the dawn which promised fair — to which a groaning world turned in hope, but he did not live to see the night that ushered in in ruin and blood ; he saw the tyrants in dismay—he was spared from seeing the patriots weeping in despair !

Added, therefore, to all his poverty and toil, he is made to know by those who paid

his pittance, that the iron shackles of slavery
are rivetted on his soul; and he for whom
heaven and earth and mankind were but one
vast home, is informed by the Powers in
high places, that " his business is not to
think ;" — *he,* the very condition of whose
existence was thought—in whose fine imagination there was ever springing up new
forms of truth and beauty. If a being must
say nothing but what he is taught, and
make no movements but that to which his
keepers train him — then, in the name of
nature and reason, choose animals suited to
the purpose : choose the parrot and the
monkey; but leave man *that* without which
his life is a lie against his origin and his
destiny. Take the eagle from the blue sky,
his pinions are unnerved and his eye grows
dim ;—take the lion from his fenceless plain,
and his majesty is gone ; — deprive man of
free thought and free speech, and you leave
him little else that is worth preserving.

Burns, in the latter years of his life, had
mortifications to endure that must have fallen
heavily on his high and manly nature. The

keenest cut adversity can give is, when it
exposes a generous spirit to the petty sneer
of wealthy and ignorant vanity. From such
insults there is no refuge ; and though those
who offer them can occasion pain, they are
yet below contempt and unworthy of revenge.
It came low indeed with the poet of Scotland,
when such creatures dared to cross his path.
Yet little great people came to look coldly on
the author of " Tam o' Shanter," and " The
Cotter's Saturday Night." Does not every
honest cheek feel hot with shame, and every
right heart feel stung with anger to read of
such an incident as the following ?—

"Mr. Mc Culloch, of Ardwell," says
Allen Cunningham, " has been heard to
relate that, on visiting Dumfries one fine
evening, to attend a ball given during the
races, he saw Burns walking on the south
side of the 'plain stanes,' while the central
part was crowded with ladies and gentlemen,
drawn together for the festivities of the night.
Not one of them took any notice of the poet ;
on which Mr. Mc Culloch went up to him,
took his arm, and wished him to join the

gentry. ' Nay, nay,' he said, ' that is all
over with me now.' "

> " O, were we young, as we once hae been,
> We should hae been galloping down on yon green,
> And lilting it over the lily white lea,—
> And were na my heart light, I wad die."

But the hand of early death was soon to
lay his follies and his miseries in the silent
grave. It is painful to read Currie's eloquent
and pathetic account of his closing hours.
His constitution, naturally sensitive and sus-
ceptible to a high degree, was, in addition,
kept in ceaseless and preternatural excitement
by the use of stimulants. How does not
every pure mind feel for the fall of the
noble! How does not one's nature lead him
to mourn and weep in bitter tears over
sunken and low-lying genius ! " From Oct.,
1792," Currie says, " to January following,
an accidental complaint confined him to the
house. A few days after he began to go
abroad he dined at a tavern, and returned
home about three o'clock very cold, numbed,
and intoxicated." Now the truth is, that
there is no splendour of talent which can
conceal the degradation of a position like

E

this : alas ! if it be so with Burns, who
had the glow of heavenly fire within him,
which could never be utterly extinguished,
what must it be in those who have nothing
to redeem their sottishness and debasement?
" In all his waywardness," Dr. Currie tells
us, " Burns met nothing in his domestic
circle but gentleness and forgiveness, except
in the gnawings of his own remorse. He
acknowledged his transgressions to the wife
of his bosom,— promised amendment,— and
again and again received pardon. But as
the strength of his body decayed, his resolu-
tion became feebler, and habit acquired pre-
dominant strength." To know into what
agonies remorse could sometimes plunge him,
we have only to refer to the shuddering words
in which the following letter is written, in
apology for an instance of irregularity : " I
write you," he says, " from the regions of
hell, and amid the horrors of the damned.
Here am I laid on a bed of pittiless torture,
while an internal tormentor, wrinkled and
cruel, called Recollection, with a whip of
scorpions, forbids peace or rest to approach

me, and keeps anguish perpetually awake.
I wish to be reinstated in the good opinion
of the fair circle whom my conduct last night
so much offended."

The physical constitution of Burns was now
in truth shattered beyond recovery, and every
effort to restore it proved in vain. In dining
with one of his female friends, whom he
observed struck with his worn appearance,
he said " Well, madam, have you got any
commands for the other world!" The ac-
counts of others are sufficiently affecting; but
they are tales of gladness, compared with the
views which Burns' own letters give of the
gloomy circumstances which darkened the
closing period of his life. They are heart-
rending compositions. They seem as if written
with the blackest drops of misery; with the
very lees of misfortune;—the darkest and
bitterest gall of his despair. Read, for ex-
ample, one of his latest letters to Thompson,
whom he had furnished with some of his best
songs. " Alas! I fear it will be some time
ere I tune my lyre again. By Babel's streams
I have sat and wept ever since I saw you last.

I have only known existence by the pressure of the heavy hand of sickness; and have counted time by the repercussions of pain. Rheumatism, cold, and fever, have formed to me a terrible combination. I close my eyes in misery, and open them without hope: I look on the vernal day, and say with poor Ferguson—

> ' Say, wherefore has an all-indulgent Heaven
> Light to the comfortless and wretched given!'"

Writing for the loan of ten pounds to an intimate friend, near the end of his days, he thus pleads: "Forgive me this earnestness, but the terrors of a jail have made me half distracted." To his brother, about the same time, he writes: "God keep my wife and children; if I am taken from them, they will be poor indeed. Remember me to my mother." But I am not aware of ever having met with any composition which so harrowed every melancholy feeling as his last letter to Mrs. Dunlop, an old high-born lady, whom Burns revered because he saw in her the blood of Wallace, and who returned his respect by admiration of his genius. "I have

written so often," he says, " and without re-
ceiving any answer, that I would not trouble
you again, but for the circumstances in which
I am. An illness which has long hung about
me will speedily send me beyond that bourn
whence no traveller returns. Your friendship
with which for many years you honoured me
was a friendship dearest to my soul. Your
conversation, and especially your correspon-
dence, were at once highly entertaining and
instructive. With what pleasure did I use
to break up the seal! The rememberance
adds one pulse more to my poor palpitating
heart. Farewell!" This letter was written
nine days before his death, and is supposed
to be his latest composition.

The English Government refused his hum-
ble request for full pay,—refused it to a dying
poet, and an indigent family. It is no glory
to the memory of Pitt, that the last years of
poor Burns were darkened under his admin-
istration, with a harshness and a rigour that
tracked him to his death. When this heaven-
born statesman—as his adorers loved to call
him—allowed genius to writhe under the

goad of penury, he was dispensing pensions
to profligate paupers; he was distributing
secret service-money to hirelings and traitors,
who would betray their fathers for a mess of
pottage; and he was spending millions in
wars which have left us our enormous Nation-
al Debt! Yet, after all Burns' frailties, and
under such depression as has rarely hung over
a death-bed, the poet was true to himself, and
his sentiments were noble to the last. "The
partiality of my countrymen," he says, (in
writing to one of his aristocratic friends,)
"has brought me forward as a man of genius,
and has given me a character to support."
"In the poet," says Dr. Currie, " I have
avowed manly and independent sentiments,
which I trust will be found in the man. My
honest fame is my dearest concern. Burns,"
he continues, "was a poor man by birth, and
an exciseman by necessity, but I will say it—
the sterling of his honest worth no poverty
could debase; and his independent British
mind oppression might bend but could not
subdue." Shortly after this, Burns, in the
thirty-eighth year of his age, quitted a world

that was not soon to look upon his like again. Burns, the gladdener of many hearts, was at last out-wrestled by a sorrow which was too strong for him;—Burns, who has deeply felt all the rapture of genius, and all the miseries of life;—Burns, in whose poetry there was so much sweetness, in whose experience there was so much sorrow!

It is in truth a sad and eventful tale, over which to weep, to ponder, and to learn; mingled as it is with so much queerness, eccentricity, and farce, but deepening at last with the most painful tragedies. The moral is on the face of the story. If happiness could have been secured by one of the loftiest and truest muses that ever sung;—if happiness could have found a resting place in one of the most honest hearts that ever struck against a manly bosom;—if happiness were the necessary companion of an eloquence that never failed, of an imagination that was as rich as the bosom of Nature, and as bright as the stars in heaven;—if happiness could have been brought down from the sky by noble and aspiring sentiments, and fixed upon earth by generous and gentle affections,—*then* happiness would have dwelt with Burns. But, unfortunately, Burns had in addition, habits to which peace soon becomes a stranger; and whoever has such habits—be he Bard, or be he beggar,—may look for the evil day at no distant date; in all the bitterness of his spirit, and for ever, he may say—

"Farewell! the tranquil mind!"

But in judging of Burns, and in judging of others similar, the caution of Dr. Currie is worthy of all imitation. "It is indeed," he observes, "a duty to the living, not to allow our admiration of great genius, or even our pity for its unhappy destiny, to conceal or disguise its errors. But there are sentiments of respect, and even of tenderness, with which this duty should be performed; there is an awful sacredness which invests the sanctity of the dead, and let those who would moralise over the grave of their contemporaries, reflect with humility on their own errors, nor forget how soon they may themselves require the candour and the sympathy they are called on to bestow."

But there is no moral drawn from the life of Burns by any writer so impressive and so eloquent as that which he has drawn himself, with a kind of melancholy prophecy, whilst he was in the full blaze of his genius and his glory. It is " The Bard's Epitaph." How sad and foreboding is its whole spirit, and how true also! —

"Is there a whim-inspired fool,
Owre fast for thought, owre hot for rule,
Owre blate to seek, owre proud to snool,
    Let him draw near;
And owre this grassy heap sing dool,
    And drap a tear.

" Is there a bard of rustic song,
Who, noteless, steals the crowds among,
That weekly this area throng,
    Oh, pass not by!
But, with a frater-feeling strong,
    Here, heave a sigh.

"Is there a man, whose judgment clear,
Can others teach the course to steer,
Yet runs, himself, life's mad career,
    Wild as the wave?
Here pause—and, through the starting tear,
    Survey this grave!

" The poor inhabitant below,
Was quick to learn, and wise to know,
And keenly felt the friendly glow,
    And softer flame;

But thoughtless follies laid him low,
      And stained his name!

"Reader, attend—whether thy soul
Soars fancy's heights beyond the pole,
Or darkling grubs this earthly hole,
      In low pursuit;
Know, prudent, cautious, self-control
      Is wisdom's root!"